AMY PLEB ANI

WRITTEN BY

DIXON BURNS

To GRANGE MOOR
Primary ScHooL
Best wishes
Dixon Burns.

CIRCA SEPTEMBER 2012

A SPECIAL THANK YOU FOR
THE LOVE AND SUPPORT OF
MY FRIENDS AND FAMILY

AMY PLEB AND THE SECRET TREE

COPYRIGHT © 2012 – DIXON BURNS

COVERS AND ILLUSTRATIONS

BY

JADE HODGSON

The woods here are full of harmony.

They hold many secrets and wonders.

The Woods are dark and tangled.

Their creatures are many.

Their pathways are winding and over

grown.

The woods here are full of mystery.

Full of Myths and Legends.

They hold secrets from ages past.

When man and forest were one.

And life was simple.

Soon a Child will learn their secrets.

But no matter how good the child.

The Secrets will be shared.

And suddenly the balance of the forest will

be shattered.

And harmony will have to be restored.

AMY PLEB AND THE SECRET TREE
CHAPTER ONE

It was Christmas Eve and Amy was very excited. It was not only the day before she would find out what great presents she would be getting, but also her Uncle Lawless was coming to stay with them for Christmas.

Everything had been prepared. The Christmas tree which Amy's dad Arthur had bought that day had already been decorated by an eager Amy, helped by her mum Calamity.

The Goose and the vegetables were all ready to be cooked for Christmas dinner. The food that they would eat that evening was all ready which included cold Gammon, Stand Pie, pickles and an assortment of nibbles.

The smell of the Christmas tree filled the whole

house and there was a roaring fire in the lounge. Amy's pet cat Tilly was layed on the rug next to the fire. This was her favourite place in the whole house in the winter time.

It was very cold outside and it had been snowing on and off, for the most part of the day. The lounge and other downstairs rooms were lavishly decorated and Amy was looking forward to her eleventh Christmas.

It was about six o'clock and it had gone dark by the time Uncle Lawless arrived. It had taken him some time to get there because he had been finishing off a painting for a client and the journey had taken longer than normal due to the driving conditions in the bad weather.

Never the less he arrived carrying his bags with him. He was greeted by a very excited Amy who flung herself at Lawless before he could drop his bags at the door. She was closely followed by Calamity.

Amy held Lawless very tightly around his waist. "Missed you," she said.

"Missed you too sweetheart."

Amy then let go and pulled back from Lawless saying in a perplexed voice "what took you so long? I've been waiting for you for two hours."

"I am sorry Amy but I had deadlines to meet, and the weather is not good. Anyway I'm here now."

Calamity went to her brother and gave him a hug and a kiss.

Lawless told Amy and Calamity that Shambles sent his love.

Just then Arthur walked in the hallway from the Kitchen and offered his right hand to Lawless who reached out and shook it.

"How ya doing mate?" Arthur said.

"Ok Arthur" replied Lawless. "How are you?"

"Fine mate." Arthur replied back.

Lawless addressed all three saying Shambles sent his best wishes.

"How is he?" asked Amy eagerly.

"He's fine love. He asked me to give you this."

Lawless reached into his jacket pocket and produced a small book and handed it to Amy. Amy looked at it and realised that it was book of poetry. Amy was surprised as it was a very fancy looking book with gold braid on it and it appeared to be very old.

"It's great uncle Lawless."

"Read what's inside the front cover."

Amy opened it and looked inside. There was some writing on it from Shambles hand.

It read all my love from Shambles. God Bless you Amy. I hope you enjoy the book.

Calamity then asked Amy to show her uncle to the guest bedroom. Amy did so and a few moments later they were both upstairs. Lawless was unpacking and Amy helped.

"I have something to tell you Amy," said Lawless. "What?" Amy asked.

"Well Amy you know that me and your mum were brought up in Cogan?"
"Yes."

"Well I know Cogan like the back of my hand and tonight I want to take you to a very special place.

But it is a secret Amy and no one must know about it. So you must promise not to tell anyone."
"Not even my parents?" Amy asked.

"Your mum and dad know, but they can keep the

secret. But I do not want you tell anyone else. Nobody, not your best friend or anyone."

"Ok" Amy replied.

"Anyway Amy I know I can trust you because you have kept the secret of Shambles."

"Yes Uncle Lawless I have and I always will." Just then Calamity called up to the pair shouting "come on down you two, there's drinks and food on the go."

Both of them stopped what they were doing and went downstairs.

As they got downstairs they went into the kitchen where Arthur thrust a large glass of beer into Lawless's hand.

"There mate get ya laughing gear round that."

"Cheers Arthur." Lawless took a large gulp of the beer. "That's great."

Arthur picked his glass up and said cheers too. Then he took an even larger gulp saying "boy I needed that."

Amy said "can I have a drink Dad?" Arthur said nothing but reached to the side board and gave Amy a tall glass of juice.

"Thanks dad."

Calamity said "right guys we'll have a couple of drinks then we'll have some food."

After their meal the four sat in the lounge and played party games. They joked, laughed and made merry.

Normally in the Pleb household on Christmas Eve if Amy was still awake they would go to Midnight mass. But this year Lawless had taken Calamity to one side and told her that he wanted to take Amy to the secret place.

Calamity had agreed after squaring it with Arthur. But she told Lawless that they must be back as quickly as possible because Amy had to go to bed and sleep as another very special guest would be visiting the Pleb residence that night.

All be it Santa Clause of course.

CHAPTER TWO

At about eleven thirty they all put on their jackets, scarves and gloves and ventured out into the cold. Calamity and Arthur made their way to Cogan church in the village for Midnight mass and Lawless and Amy took off in the other direction. But not before promising Calamity they would come back soon so Amy could go to bed.

They both agreed and went off on their merry way.

Amy was not sure what would happen next or where Lawless would take her but she trusted him very much and knew that he would not lead her astray or into any danger.

Although it had been snowing intermittently for a few hours, the snow had now stopped and the sky was clear and stars had appeared in the night sky.

The moon was out and it was almost full. Lawless led Amy down the road to the side of the Fogan River.

It was quite wide, deep and normally fast flowing but tonight it was Icy and Amy thought she would not like to fall in, as it would be very cold indeed. They walked along the side of the river for a few minutes, and then they came to the foot bridge. They crossed over the river turning right and continued walking on to another small road which eventually turned into a dirt road and then narrowed into a path.

Amy had never been this way before or if she had

it had never been at night and in the freezing cold. But despite this she was very excited and wondered what she would find at the end of their journey and what surprise her uncle had in store for her.

The pair then walked down the path for a couple of minutes and came to a fence. Lawless bounced over it closely followed by Amy. They ended up in a field and Lawless lead them across. It was well lit by moonlight and they could each see their way.

They went to the other side of the field and came to a dry stone wall. Lawless made his way across a broken down section of the wall and he offered his right hand to Amy so she could walk across safely.

Amy then found herself at the edge of a dark and overgrown wood. There was very little light to start with and Amy became quite frightened. She whispered to Lawless that she was scared. Lawless squeezed her hand and whispered back "don't be scared love you'll be fine."

Amy then found courage in her Uncles words and she followed him like a lamb. Lawless lead them up a path and this became steeper and steeper and windier and windier and more and more slippery under foot, which was due to the Icy conditions.

The wood was still very dark and despite her eyes becoming used to this she still found it difficult to walk. Eventually the path ended and Amy and Lawless found themselves in a clearing in the wood. The clearing was covered in snow and Amy could see better now. She noticed a Tree in the centre of the clearing.

Amy tugged at Lawless jacket sleeve and whispered "what is this place?"

Lawless replied. "It's One Tree Wood."

CHAPTER THREE

"Why One Tree Wood?" Amy asked.

Lawless replied "can you see that tree stood over there on its own?"

"Yes."

The light shone on the Clearing and Amy could see the tree very plainly. It was a fir Tree. It stood about seven feet tall and it was very much like the one Amy had in her lounge back home.

"Is this the secret place you told me about?" Amy whispered.

"Yes Amy it is."

"You've brought me to see a tree?"

"Not just a tree Amy."

Amy felt a little let down and a bit fed up after being dragged out on such a cold night to stand in a dark wood, staring at a tree with just Uncle Lawless for company.

Amy asked "can we go home now? I'm cold." Amy also felt a bit scared.

She whispered again to Lawless. "I'm cold and a bit scared too."

"Don't be scared love."

Lawless looked at his watch. It was about three minutes to midnight.

Just then Amy and Lawless heard a rustling of leaves and foliage. All of a sudden animals of all sizes from Voles and rabbits to deer's, even fox's began to appear in the clearing.

They must have all been awoken from their winter sleep.

Amy felt even more uneasy but Lawless reassured her saying "they won't harm you Amy."

Lawless looked at his watch again it was exactly twelve midnight and as the church bells chimed Amy noticed the tree light up as if someone had turned on some fairy lights.

Amy whispered to Lawless "who turned the lights on?"

"Nobody did Amy."

"How did it light up then?"

"I don't know myself love, it just does. Every year at this time it lights up as if by magic."

As time went on the lights shone brighter and brighter and just then Amy noticed all the animals kneel down.

"What are they doing Uncle Lawless" Amy whispered?

"I don't know Amy they always do this. It's as if their paying homage to the tree."

After two minutes the animals rose to their feet and began to chant in their own respective tongues. Which began softly and became louder and louder until it was an almost deafening chant.

Amy thought that the sound they were making sounded like they were speaking English. She thought it sounded like Winter man come, Winter man come.

Amy asked Lawless "who's the Winter man?" Lawless told Amy that he is the Guardian of the forest and appears every year.

He keeps the forest safe and he is the protector of the tree.
Suddenly the animals stopped their chanting and the clearing fell silent once more.

Just then snow began to fall on the clearing and then there appeared to be some

movement from the ground at the foot of the tree.
The snow began to move and suddenly a snowy
figure arose from the ground.

Lawless Whispered to himself "The Winter man."

Amy looked at him in wonder.

He was covered in Ice and snow. He took the
form of a Tree. He had a trunk like body, two smaller
trunks for legs and branches formed his arms. His
fingers were twigs and his feet were thick tangled
roots. He stood about six feet tall. His face was like
entwined twigs covered in moss. His ears leaves and
his lips and eye brows were twigs and his eyes were

wide, wild, white and icy. They bulged from his head and shone like two bright diamonds.

And Amy thought that even if the moon had not been out that night she would still have been able to see them.

Just then the Winter man bent forward and picked up a stick from the ground, which was about three feet long.

He took the stick and put it to his lips and blew into it. It made a shrill piercing sound.

The animals knelt again this time in silence and the only sound that could be heard was the sound of the Winter man blowing the simple wooden instrument for all he was worth. As he blew out a clear and simple tune which Amy had never heard before, the Winter man began to dance around the tree. Slowly at first but as the tune gathered pace, so did he. He began to prance and leap into the air.

He leaped and pirouetted in the winter moonlight around the tree faster and faster. The snow flew up around his root like feet. He kicked into the air with his right foot and then his left. The animals began to chant again Winter man, Winter man, over and over.

This went on for about five minutes but it seemed like an eternity to Amy. The tune became louder and louder, wilder and wilder, and the chanting louder and louder. The Winter man still prancing, dancing and whirling around the illuminated tree, in wild abandon.

Just then the animals stopped their chant. The Winter man continued to play unaccompanied. His playing became even more wild and erratic. Then suddenly the pace began to get slower and slower and the tune became softer and softer and fainter and fainter. The dancing slowed and turned into a walk around the tree.

He made his last circuit around the tree and blew his last note, as the stick moved from his lips he flung it high into the air. It dropped back to earth like a stone back into his right twig like hand and he flung it into to the ground only to be engulfed by snow.

The Winter man then fell backwards into the snow from where he had sprung and disappeared under the snow, as quickly as he had appeared.

As the Winter man was layed to rest again for another year, the light from the tree got fainter and fainter and suddenly the light faded for another year. Just as the light went out the animals dispersed and disappeared back into the wood.

Amy could not believe her eyes or ears. There seemed to be little point in her trying to tell anyone about this as no one would ever believe her anyway.

She could not even believe it and she had just seen it for herself.

She turned to Lawless and said "that was wonderful."

"It was," Lawless replied.

"But how does this happen? Why?"

"I don't know Amy. It happens every year."

"How do you know about this place?"

"I came here with your Granddad Blanket and your mum when I was twelve and your mum was eight years old."

"So she knows everything about this place? The tree and the Winter man?"

"Yes Amy."

"Why didn't she bring me up here?"

"I agreed to bring you because your mum wanted me to."

CHAPTER FOUR

Amy and Lawless made their way back to Amy's House, leaving the tree and the clearing behind. Before they left the clearing Amy looked back at the tree thinking what a great time she had had listening to the Winter man blow his stick like instrument and hearing that shrill sound, whilst he danced and pranced around the wonderful tree and the sound of the chanting the Animals had made.

"Bye tree" Amy said in a whisper.

The pair walked back down the winding track, which was now very slippery and dark as the light from the moon was now obscured by cloud and snow was falling again.

Amy asked Lawless about six times to tell her about how her Grandad Blanket had brought him and her mum to the clearing. And six times he repeated it.

By the sixth time they were back at Amy's house. They went into the hallway and were greeted by Amy's excited Parents who had heard them come down the garden path.

Calamity went straight up to Amy and gave her a large hug and kiss.

"So you're home are you?"

"Yes mum" replied Amy.

"We're both glad. Aren't we dad?"

Arthur replied "yes we are."

"I'll make you some hot chocolate and then you can tell me what happened." But Calamity being a mum said "then you go to bed."

"But mum!" Complained Amy.

"No buts" Amy Arthur said. "You know who's

supposed to be coming to visit later. And you know very well that he won't come if a certain someone is not asleep."

"I know Dad, Santa."

"Yes Amy Santa. Now upstairs and get ready for bed, clean your teeth and then you can come down and have a drink."

Amy ran upstairs to do what was asked of her. She hurriedly came back down stairs where a hot drink was waiting for her as promised. The four sat in the lounge and Amy told her parents all about the events of the evening. When she had finished her story which was repeated at least three times, Calamity noticed that Amy was appearing tired. Her head was leaning to one side and her eyes were bleary.

Calamity then said to her "right love it's bed time

Santa won't come if you are still awake."

Calamity said this to Amy but she was not sure if Amy still believed in Santa Clause by the fact that she seemed to be asking more questions about Santa and seemed to be less convinced that a large man could climb down a chimney or even enter a house without a chimney. But then Calamity thought to herself that if Amy had seen a Tree light up, animals chant and a tree like creature rise up from the ground blowing into a stick and prancing around, she could certainly believe in Santa Clause.

Amy got up from her seat in the lounge and proceeded to kiss her mum and dad.

Uncle lawless went upstairs with Amy and put her to bed. He kissed her good night and then she whispered to him, "It was real wasn't it uncle lawless? "What I saw tonight?"

"Yes Amy it was. Go to sleep now," Lawless said, "shall I switch the bed side light off?"

"No" replied Amy.

"Ok love I'll see you in the morning."

Lawless left Amy's room shutting the door behind him and returned to the lounge to finish his drink.

Meanwhile Amy lay in bed thinking that she would never sleep again after what had just happened. But after a few minutes Amy was fast asleep.

Amy's parents and Lawless remained downstairs for about half an hour then they all retired to bed.

The rest of Christmas was great for Amy and her family. Christmas morning was wonderful with Amy opening all her lovely presents and in the afternoon eating the extravagant feast that was Christmas Dinner.

But there was one thing that she would never

forget, when she was standing in the clearing with her uncle, watching the Tree light up, with all the animals of the forest chanting and the Winter man prancing, dancing and playing to his heart's content. Amy thought it was the best Christmas she had ever had.

CHAPTER FIVE

Almost twelve months had past, since Amy's great Christmas. She was now eleven years old, and she was growing up fast. Both Arthur and Calamity noticed a change in her.

She was more confident, forthright and independent than ever before.

Amy was doing well at school and soon would be leaving primary school.

Since her experience in One Tree Wood last Christmas, Amy had been reading about the history surrounding the tree and that of the Winter man. Uncle Lawless had sent her a book called Mysteries of the Forest by Donald Blackspot. A famous local historian and author, who had lived in the Cogan area for many years. He had died in 1907 and the book was now out of print and copies were very hard to come by.

The Book delved into the history and mystery surrounding woodland areas. She had read a chapter about the Winter man and how he was considered to be the guardian of the woods who holds on to the winter and helps to fight off the spring, until winter finally succumbs to it.

Amy had found a song in the Book which appeared to describe what she had witnessed last Christmas Eve.

The song of the Winter man

The Winter man blows out his rhyme.

He prances and dances in double quick time.

He pivots and pirouettes around the tree.

Paying no heed to me nor thee.

He plays his tune with Gusto and Glee.

In deference to his beloved tree.

The Creatures chant knelt around the tree.

Paying no heed to me nor thee.

They ball and bleat with gusto and glee.

In deference to their beloved tree.

Winter man leaps and bounds in one tree wood.

So the Evil world can at last be good.

He prances and dances round one tree wood.

So naughty children can at last be good.

The Creatures chant in one tree wood.

So the evil world can at last be good.

They ball and rant in one tree wood.

So the naughty children can at last be good.

The Tree Glows and shines in one tree wood.

So the evil world can at last be good.

It lights up the night in one tree wood.

So naughty children can at last be good.

When winter man comes to blow his last.

He pays his dues to future and past.

He blows his last note slow and low.

Then falls back into the fallen snow.

The Tree then glows its last.

After paying its dues to future and past.

The tree glows bright and glows no more.

But returns every year brighter than before.

The Winter man blows and blows no more

But returns the next year louder than before.

The Creatures bleat and bleat no more

But return next year bleating all the more.

Amy had read the book from cover to cover and

she was itching to get back up into the wood again on

Christmas Eve to watch the Winter man perform, see

the tree glow in the dark and hear the woodland

Animals chant.

Despite Amy becoming engrossed in reading about One Tree Wood and the Winter man, Amy was not letting it rule her life like storms once did.

She was still as popular with everyone. And of course boys were taking a serious interest in her, which in turn helped to boost her confidence even further.

Infact she had been asked out by practically every eligible lad in the school. She had been asked out by Harry Compton on a monday lunchtime in November and he blew her out on the Wednesday. The reason was not that Amy could not hold on to her beau but that he appeared to be the Schools serial dater and asked girls out for the fun of the chase and dumped them a few days later. Amy was at first saddened by this but after a talk to her dad, who just said "ya best off without him duck," she cheered up and came to her senses.

One such lad had taken a real shine to Amy, infact they had known each other for some time.
The boy was called Radley Banks and he and Amy had known each other since their pre-school days, when each of them went to the same child minders. They had been friends for all that time too.

Radley was a nice lad or at least this is what Amy thought. He too was very popular with peers and teachers alike. He was not much of a Scholar but he was athletic and he was always playing sports of any kind. He played Football in the Winter and Cricket in the summertime. He was a good all-rounder and had a good top spin.

Radley had asked Amy to be his girlfriend and they were now going steady so to speak. But being eleven, only hand holding allowed.

It was three days before Christmas and Amy was looking forward to Christmas again. But she was a little sad too because Uncle Lawless would not be staying with them this year. Due to the fact that he was in Australia doing some landscape painting up in the Northern Territory.

Lucky him Amy thought, but he would miss out because he would not see the Winter man this year.

Amy had broken up from school a couple of days before and she and Radley had agreed to meet up before Christmas.

It was the twenty second of December and that morning Radley had called for her and they went for a walk. The weather was cold and there was a fresh fall of snow. But they were dressed warmly.

As they walked Radley and Amy had been talking about secrets they each had. Radley seemed to have this idea that if they told each other their most precious secrets then their relationship would somehow be stronger.

Radley had a secret that he was itching to share with Amy. And Amy herself clearly had a secret, two infact. One was Shambles and the Tall Tower over in Fogan. And of course she had an even bigger secret standing in One Tree Wood.

Amy felt very reluctant to tell Radley either of her secrets. It was not that she did not trust him. She did very much so. They had been friends for years.

She was concerned that if those secrets were somehow exposed then this could put Shambles at risk and the tree and the Winter man himself. Either way Amy had a dilemma on her hands.

But Amy felt a strong compulsion to tell her secret because Radley seemed to be banging on about it a lot. Even at some point being heavy handed about it, almost manipulative.

Well if you don't tell me you're secret then you're not my friend, that kind of thing.

Radley went ahead anyway and told her his secret as they walked and talked, through the winter landscape.

It was a place. It was a place where he would go particularly in the spring and the summertime. It was a cave he let upon last summer.

The cave was in a large disused quarry. He lead her through the snow strewn fields and then through a wood. They walked up a long path and came to a gate which they scaled. Once over the gate, they walked down another path through a small row of trees.

Just then they came upon the large quarry. Radley led Amy down the winding path to the bottom of the quarry. Amy was a bit scared because the path was steep and uneven under their feet. The path was slippery too due to the snow and some ice.

But Amy thought to herself if she could walk up to one tree wood in the middle of the night in total darkness like last year, then this was a piece of cake for her. And with this thought her uneasiness left her. At least she could see.

After the unsteady climb down the path, the pair reached the base of the Quarry, where Radley asked Amy to close her eyes. He took her by her right arm and then led her to his secret place.

The cave entrance was hidden by a large bolder which had fallen from the top of the Quarry many years ago. This was good because from a distance no one would notice if the cave was there or not.

This was Radley's den, his special place, a place

where he could come when he was sad or upset, or when he had had a bust up with his dad.

His dad was always nagging him about something or other.

It was a place where he felt safe and could hide away whenever his dad kicked off with his mum. He would come here when his dad was angry or drunk, which these days was quite often.

Radley asked Amy to open her eyes and she did so. She slowly looked around the cave, which was dimly lit by a paraffin lamp that Radley had lit just before Amy had opened her eyes.

She was amazed. She had never seen a den like this before. It reminded her of Aladdin's cave, and she half expected a Genie to pop out of the paraffin lamp which was resting on an orange box which acted as a make shift table.

"This is great Radley" said Amy. "When will the Genie appear?"

Radley laughed.

"Do you really like it Amy?"

"Yes Rad I do." This was her nickname for him.

The couple sat down on the large make shift chair Radley had made from a large log, three planks of wood and an old carpet.

They sat there chatting to each other and taking in the occasion.

It was cold but they did not notice it that much. After about half an hour they left the cave and took the long twisting path back up to the top of the quarry.

Radley escorted Amy home, saying he would visit her tomorrow and she could then tell him her secret.

Amy agreed but was still a little reluctant to let him into her little secret but then she thought what harm could it do. She trusted Radley as he had trusted her with his favourite place, the place which to Radley was his place of refuge, whenever things got rough at home.

"I'll see you tomorrow Radley and I will tell you to my secret."

"Ok I'll call for you tomorrow at about 10 O' clock."

"Ok" Amy said.

Again that evening Amy was still in two minds as to what secret she would share with him. She could not take him to the Tall Tower anyway because this was twenty miles away in Fogan. She would only be able to take him to see One Tree Wood. So to her it would be the tree that she would take him to see.

And she felt in her heart of hearts that she could trust him. But despite this Uncle Lawless words kept repeating in her ears.

"Promise me you will never tell anyone. Promise me you will never tell anyone."

His words kept resounding in her head. But Radley she told herself was not just anyone. He was her friend and she was sure that she could trust him. But she still found it difficult to sleep much that night with all that going around in her head.

But eventually despite her head going around and around she did drop off to sleep.

CHAPTER SIX

The next morning which was the twenty third of December, Amy awoke refreshed and ready to make a decision. Despite her Uncles wishes she would share her secret with Radley. And so when he came to call upon her, she was eager to let him know all about the tree and its whereabouts. But she would not let him into the fact that it was a magic tree and that the Winter man slept at its feet until Christmas Eve.

So soon after Radley arrived to collect her they were off out informing Calamity that they were going out but would not be too long. But on the way, Amy made Radley swear on his secret place that he would never tell anyone about her secret.

Radley swore to her that he would never tell a living sole. Neither his family nor his friends. And this was good enough for Amy. And so it was that Radley did keep his promise but despite his promise being kept events would unfold which would test their friendship.

And so they set off to One Tree Wood. Amy led him up the snowy icy path through the wood to the clearing.

Before they entered the wood Amy asked Radley to close his eyes. She led him with eyes shut to the centre of the clearing. She led him to where he would see the tree as soon as he opened his eyes.

"Ok you can open your eyes now."
Radley's eyes caught sight of the lonely tree.

"There" Amy said, this is my secret.
Radley looked at the tree, thinking to himself what's all the fuss about it's just a tree.

"Do you like it Radley?" This is my tree, my

special place in the whole world. I come here a lot. I like it here.

"It's great" said Radley.

Just thinking it was a tree in a wood. Not a place like his cave, a special den. But being as fond as he was of Amy he could never let on to her that he did not share her love for the place or the tree.

Radley may have been more interested to know that as the church bells strike midnight on Christmas Eve, the tree would light up and the creatures of the forest would rise from their winter sleep, chanting away to their hearts content and the Winter man would strut his stuff. But Amy was not prepared to share this with Radley. Showing him the tree was one thing but telling him it had special powers was another.

After about ten minutes Amy and Radley left the

clearing and went back into Cogan. Radley escorted Amy back home. Radley said he would see her after Christmas and would call for her. Amy agreed and they parted company.

On the way home Radley called off at the house of Johnny Camps, who was his bestest friend, second only to Amy. He played with Johnny for a couple of hours. But all the time he was at Johnny's, he never told him where he had been and who he had been with.

Upon leaving Johnny's Radley made his way home through the snowy lanes of Cogan. Radley got back to his house about one pm.

Radley went through the front door of his house hearing raised angry voices. He knew these voices only too well.

It was those of his parents Danny and Gertrude.

They were of course arguing again. And his dad was shouting the loudest.   It was a sound all too familiar in the Banks household.

Radley thought to himself, he's at it again. What's up this time?   Radley knew that his mum did not start the arguments in their house, it was his dad.   He knew only too well that he would be having a go at his mum for some reason or another and it would always be her fault never his own.

He walked into the lounge. He caught sight of his mum sat on the settee crossed legged and arms folded and sat with her head down.

His dad Danny was stood over her, shouting at her. Saying "I told you we should have bought one earlier."

"Ya know I like a proper tree at Christmas. You told me there'd be plenty but no."

"I know, I know Danny" Gertrude replied. "I knew it would be my fault!"

"Would ya listen no?" Danny shouted.

"Aren't there any other places you can go?"

"I've been to ten different places but nothing."
"I went to Bennits farm shop and they had just sold the last one to Arthur Pleb."

Radley pricked his ears up. That was Amy's dad. Danny kept ranting on and on about Arthur taking the last tree.

"I don't like him I never have."

Gertrude said "he's Amy's dad isn't he Radley?"

"Yes Mum."

She said "you've been to see her today haven't you?" Hoping to change the subject.

"Yes Mum."

But this did not change anything and Danny still kept

on complaining.

And then he said to Gertrude "why do you always change the subject when I'm talking, you do it every time?"

"I'm sorry" Gertrude said.

"Not as sorry as I am."

"It's not the end of the world Danny we can always get the artificial tree out of the loft."

"No! Not on your life."

"Why not dad Radley chirped up?"

"You shut up! I'm not talking to you, who asked you to butt in? You always butt in when I'm talking to your mother. It's none of your business anyway. Get upstairs."

Radley obeyed his dad, straight away. He knew from painful experience not to argue and knew only too well what could happen if he disobeyed.

His mother smiled at him as he went upstairs. Danny turned to Gertrude again and asked "why do you always let him join in?"

"I can't silence him by gagging him Danny."
"He'll get the toe of my boot if he's not careful."

"That's your answer for everything isn't Danny?"
"Shut up or I'll"

"Or you'll what?"

Upstairs Radley could hear his parents arguing and his dad bringing up everything that his mum had done wrong before.

All the old stuff, you're no good, I married beneath me. This went on for half an hour until Radley could stand no more.

He left his bedroom and made his way quietly down the stairs and without making a sound silently opened the back door.

He went round the back of the house, to the shed and opening the door got a large saw, a piece of rope and his sledge.

He headed out of the shed and up the garden, in the direction of the woods.

He made his way to One Tree Wood. His plan was to cut down Amy's tree. He knew Amy had only shown this to him today. He knew it was sacred to her and it was her pride and joy but it was only a tree and she would get over it, at least that's what he hoped.

But he didn't want another Christmas ruined. Last year Radley recalled the Turkey wasn't cooked to his dads liking and his mum got another black eye. He thought that if he did not act, this would happen again.

Radley made his way along the river side, up the path where Amy had led him to the fence.

He left the sledge and rope there and carried the saw with him over the fence. He made his way into the woods and up the steep sloping path to the edge of the wood.

He got to the clearing and he looked at the tree. The tree was standing there as if ready to be cut down. He walked over to it. He knelt down and taking the saw began to saw into it. The saw cut into it like a knife through butter. The trunk was about six inches thick and in no time at all he had sawn through it and it had fallen to the ground.

"There" he said.

But just then Radley had an over whelming feeling of shame and guilt, as he saw the tree lying on the ground.

He felt that he had betrayed his bestest friend in the whole world and he knew that when she found out she would never forgive him. And their friendship would be over.

But he put this thought to the back of his mind because all he could think about was to get the tree back home to save Christmas for himself and his mum. And to stop his mum from being on the receiving end of his father's temper.

Radley was quite a big lad for his age and playing all that sport made him very strong. But he found carrying the tree was too much for him so he dragged it. As he dragged it from the clearing he hoped that it wouldn't lose any pine needles. Luckily for him it didn't. What he did not want was to take it back to his dad with no needles on it. It would make his dad even angrier.

He got it down the path to the fence. He dragged it over the fence which took a great deal of effort but he managed it. He then picked it up and placed it on the sledge. He had to tie the stump on to the sledge and the tree being seven feet tall, most of it had to trail on the floor as he began to pull the sledge homewards.

Radley dragged the sledge behind him. The light of the day was slowly fading and soon it would be dark.

He dragged the Sledge and its cargo to his house and up the path to the front door. He left the sledge and tree on the path and went into the house, not even wiping his feet. But the house was quiet. No sound of his dad having a go at his mum. He found his mum in the Kitchen. She was sat hunched over the kitchen table.

Radley noticed that she was holding her left side with her right hand.

"Are you ok mum?"

"Yes love! I'm fine."

"Where's mi dad?"

"He's sat in the lounge, you'd better go in and say you're sorry!"

"Ok Mum." Radley had learned over the years that whether he or his mum were right or wrong, they must always say sorry to his dad. Radley went into the half lit lounge.

His dad was sat on the settee.

"Hi Dad."

"Hi son."

"Dad I've come to say sorry."

"Ok son." By this time Danny had calmed down.

"Dad."

"Ya."

"I've got a surprise for ya. Come outside."

"What for?"

"I've got a present for you!"

"Ok" Danny said as if it wasn't worth the effort but he felt guilty about his outburst and behaviour earlier that day.

He went outside and suddenly caught sight of the tree.

"Wow Radley where did you get that from?"

"I got it from the woods. Look at it dad isn't it great?"

"Yes son it is."

"Right let's get it inside and decorate it." Danny was so excited he was like a child. It was as if he was the child and Radley was the father who had brought the tree home for his son.

Danny untied the tree and grabbed it from the sledge and carried it inside.

Just then Gertrude came from the kitchen and saw Danny carrying the tree into the lounge with Radley following close behind.

"Where did you get it from Radley?"

"From the woods mum."

"You didn't steal it did you love?"

"No mum!"

Gertrude just looked at her son with deep love and silently mouthed the words "Thank you."

Radley nodded and smiled back at his mum.

There was one thing that made his life worthwhile when his dad was at his worst. It was the love and encouragement of his mum, who he loved more than anyone and would always defend.

Because he was only eleven he could not physically stand up to his dad, so instead he had to resort to guile and cunning, and had even had to resort to betraying his best friends trust in order to make things right at home and for the sake of his mum.

The only thing he could hope for now was for everything to go right, so he and his mum would be able to enjoy Christmas, unless his dad got drunk again and started another argument.

All Radley also hoped was that Amy would not go to the clearing before Christmas at least. And the other conciliation was that he would not be seeing her until after Christmas and would not have to face the music until then.

That evening after mounting the tree in a stand and helping Radley and Gertrude decorate it, Danny got ready and went to the pub. Radley and his mum stayed at home and spent a lovely evening together. Radley loved his mum with all his heart and she him.

As they sat together on the settee looking at the decorated tree, Radley told his mum of how he had got it from the wood across the river. He also told her that he had found the tree only because Amy had told him about it that very day.

He said that he was very sad because Amy had taken him there on the condition that he was never to tell anyone else, as it was her secret. He also told his mum that he was upset that he had taken the tree.

His mum then said that it was just a tree and if Amy knew why he had done what he did then she felt certain Amy would understand and forgive him.

Because Gertrude knew Amy to be a nice girl who

had been very well brought up and had a good family.

CHAPTER SEVEN

Back at Amy's house, the Plebs were getting ready for Christmas. They had just done the shopping and had just decorated the tree that Arthur had bought that day. Arthur had told Amy that they were lucky as the tree he had bought was the last one at the centre. He had nipped out of work that lunchtime to buy it.

Arthur told Amy that he had seen Radley's dad Danny there and that he did not seem best pleased because he had come for a tree and seemed pretty upset because Arthur had got the last one. He had even asked Arthur to sell it to him and that he could name his price.

But Arthur had told Danny that he was not interested. He had even offered him double the price but Arthur had refused point blank because he did not wish to disappoint his daughter.   Danny had cried

him the poor tale by saying that he did not want to

disappoint his son or wife.

But Arthur was in the same dilemma. Anyway

Danny had gone off in a huff.   "And that" as Arthur

often said, "was that." Amy thought nothing of this at

the time and just thought that Radley's dad would get

a tree from somewhere else.

Amy again as every year was looking forward to

Christmas. But this year however Uncle Lawless

would not be there.

Amy was a little apprehensive because he would

be calling them from Australia soon, to wish them a

happy Christmas. And she was feeling guilty about

how she had led Radley to the Secret Tree.

But she would have been more horrified if she

knew what had happened to the tree and the fact that

it was now standing in Radley's lounge with lights and Christmas decorations on it.

The next day was Christmas Eve and again Amy was very excited. Arthur had left early to go to work in the hope that he would be able to finish early. Calamity had finished work until after the New Year and she was getting the house ready for Christmas.

The weather had turned cold again and Arthur had to defrost his car that morning before setting off for work.

Amy and her mum had had a nice lunch and after this with her mum's permission, she had gone out for a walk. It was about two pm and the news had said that there was going to be more snow coming.

Amy had already asked her mum and dad the day before if they could go to the clearing that night before twelve midnight. But Amy wanted to go up to the tree before dark as she had a strange feeling that all was not well. She could not be sure of her feelings but just wanted to make sure. She felt sure that her secret was safe with Radley but something deep inside her was saying.

"Go and see."

"Go and see."

So this is what she did. Amy made her way along the river bank and up over the fence making her way up through the woods via the path which was very slippery and would be worse tonight.

She made her way to One Tree Wood and of course was expecting and hoping to see the tree still standing there in the clearing. But she was absolutely distraught to find that the tree had gone with just a stump left.

Amy ran from the clearing with tears in her eyes,

thinking the worst of Radley.   Thinking he had told

his friends, or worse his dad who had come up to steal

the tree because he had not been able to buy one. She

ran all the way to Radley's without stopping.

She ran to the front door and knocked on it very

loudly. Radley answered the door, with a rather

sheepish look on his face.

"Amy what do you want?"

"Someone has stolen the tree!" Amy said

hysterically.

"Stolen?"

"Yes Stolen! Someone cut it down and all that's left

is a stump!"

Radley shrugged as if he didn't know anything

about it.

But Amy could sense he was not himself and she felt

certain he knew something he was not letting on.

"What's wrong Radley?"

Radley again shrugged his shoulders.

But Amy knew something was wrong and asked "is it your dad again?"

"Yes Radley replied back."

"What has he done this time?"

"He got angry with mum again." Then he broke down telling Amy everything.

"I took the tree! I took it, Amy. It's in the lounge decorated with lights on it."

"Why" Amy asked?

"Because your dad had taken the last Christmas tree from Bennits and my dad had got really angry and took it out on mum like he always does. I think he's hit her again Amy."

"Just because he couldn't get a tree?"

"Yes Amy. He's done it before for less than that."

Radley told her about what his dad had done before.

Just then Radley's Dad came out of the house. He looked Amy up and down and asked, "what does she want?"

Radley said "nothing dad."

At this point Amy became very angry and with a raised voice said "that is my tree in there." Amy could see it partly through the lounge window.

"Not on your life girly it's ours, you've got your own."

"It doesn't belong to you or anyone it belongs to the wood. It's been there for years."

Danny just laughed in Amy's face.

"Well girl it's ours now and it's in our house and here is where it stays."

"We'll see about that" Amy said.

"What ya gonna do, get ya dad to come and beat mi up?"

 Amy ran off.

Radley was going to run after her but Danny grabbed him by the arm and said "ya going nowhere mi lad, inside now."

Radley wanted to resist but he knew it was not wise to do so when his dad was in that frame of mind.

Whilst Radley went back into the house, Amy was racing back to her house. She was running as fast as she could even with the snow on the ground. She got back home went in through the front door and flew into the kitchen where her mum was.

Calamity saw Amy she was very out of breath and doubled in two from running all the way from Radley's house.

"What on earth in the matter darling?"

Amy caught her breath and said "it's Radley, he's taken the tree from the wood!"

"What in One Tree Wood? Why? How could he have done that?"

"Because I took him up there yesterday. I got him to swear that he would never tell anyone. But he cut the tree down because his dad could not get a tree from anywhere! And to stop his dad from having a go at his mum. So he took it home and now it's in Radley's lounge with fairy lights and decorations all over it."

"Honestly some men, who do they think they are?"

"Right Calamity said to Amy. I know what we'll do. We have to go to the wood and awake the Winter man."

"How though Mum?"

"Where is the book that Uncle Lawless gave you?"

"It's in my room."

"Good go and get it quickly"

"Yes Mum"

Amy dashed upstairs she had caught her breath by now.   She returned within two minutes carrying the book.

"Here mum."

"Thanks Amy."

Calamity opened it at the page where there was a charm to wake the Winter man. She quickly read the charm and the instructions it gave.

Right Amy lets go to the wood. Calamity put on her snow boots, warm coat, scarf and gloves. They left the house with Calamity locking the door behind them. By now the day was drawing to a close and the light was fading.

They made their way up to the clearing.

As they entered the clearing despite the fading light,

Calamity could see the stump of the tree. They stood ten feet away from the stump.

Calamity wasted no time in opening the book at the right page and began to read the charm. "Amy we'll need a stick from the wood"

Amy went to the edge of the wood in search of a stick. She noticed a stick that was partially covered in snow and ice. She quickly stooped to pick it up. It was entangled with leaves and roots from other trees but it moved quickly from its position with a sharp tug from Amy's gloved right hand.

She picked up the stick, which was about four feet long and took it straight back to her mum. "Here's a stick mum."

"That's fine Amy. Now you keep hold of it while I read out the charm. But we must follow the instructions word for word."

"Naughty Child take this staff, wave it sky ward fore and aft."

"Wave it around in One Tree Wood, so naughty children can at last be good."

Amy felt uneasy about this because the charm was saying she was naughty.

"I can't do this mum."

"You have to Amy! After all you did wrong by telling Radley, and Radley did wrong for cutting down the tree. You are both to blame. And you have to make it right."

"Ok Mum I'll do it."

Calamity began to read the charm again.

"Naughty child take this staff, wave it sky ward fore and aft."

Amy took the stick and held it aloft and began to wave it back and forth.

"Wave it around in One Tree Wood, so naughty children can at last be good."

"Place the staff upon the ground, so the Winter man can hear the sound."

"Bang it thrice upon the ground, so the Winter man can hear the sound."

"Bang it hard and bang it firm so the Winter man will start to turn."

Amy took the stick and banged it on the ground three times as the charm said.

"Then with that done speak these words."

"Winter man come"

"Winter man come."

When Calamity had finished reading the charm she ushered for Amy to start chanting the words.

"Winter man come."

Amy started to chant.

"Winter man come.

Winter man come."

And Calamity joined in.

They had to repeat the charm over and over again.
They did so until the words became meaningless to
them. Amy began to think that their chanting was
hopeless and nothing would happen.

But then after a couple of minutes, they each felt a
rumble in the ground below them. And suddenly the
snow began to move and Winter man appeared,
slowly rising like he had last Christmas Eve. His tree
like body was covered in ice and snow, he shone as if
a light was shining on him. His diamond like eyes
pierced Amy's eyes.

Calamity grabbed Amy's right sleeve and started
to kneel on the ground pulling Amy with her. They
both knelt on the snowy frozen ground. The snow

penetrated their jeans and each could feel the wetness at their knees.

Then Calamity spoke to the Winter man "Good Sir a great wrong has been done. The tree has been cut down and taken from here. My daughter has done wrong sir, she told her friend and he has taken the tree away."

The Winter man turned to look to see the tree missing with only its stump remaining.
He said nothing but with his tree like legs he left the clearing.

Amy turned to her mum and said "what is he doing mum?"
"He's going to get the tree"
"Shall we follow him?"
"No we must stay here"

The Winter man made his way down the path and

into the village. Fortunately no one saw him. He would have been a frightening sight to anyone who set eyes upon him.

He went straight to Radley's House. He must have sensed where the tree was. He went down the path to the front door, opened it and went right inside without knocking. He went into the lounge and made his way to the tree which was near the bay window. He picked up the tree with his twig like right hand and pulled it from the tree stand. He shook it and the baubles fell off as if by magic. He pulled off the fairy lights and tinsel.

He walked to the lounge door but then was confronted by a wide eyed Danny. With Radley and Gertrude stood in the hallway watching. Danny stood blocking the lounge doorway. He was brandishing a baseball bat and threatened to strike him with it.

"What in God's name are you? And where do you think ya taking that?"

The Winter man stood and looked right into Danny angry eyes with his, and spoke to him in pigeon English.

"Tak tri bak ti wud."

"No you're not."

The Winter man began to walk forward making his way to the door.

Suddenly Danny raised the bat to strike the Winter man, but he grabbed the bat from Danny with his free left hand pulling it from his grasp and flung it to the other side of the room.

Danny then threw himself at the Winter man but he just bounced off him like a rubber ball. Danny felt as if he had been hit by a large lump of metal, and went flying backwards on to the hard wooden floor, striking the back of his head. He immediately fell unconscious.

The Winter man then turned to Danny, pointing his left finger at him, as he did a long streak of light like a thin strand of ice shot from the Winter man's twig like finger. A silvery spot about half an inch wide appeared on Danny's forehead where he had been struck.

The ice melted turning to water and ran down Danny's face. Danny's head jerked and wobbled for a second or two then he stopped moving.

As Danny lay on the floor, Radley came into the

lounge. Only to see the Winter man with the tree in his right hand.

"What have you done to my dad? And where are you going with our tree?"

The Winter man looked at Radley with his diamond white piercing eyes.

Gertrude followed him into the lounge to see her son stood in front of the Winter man and her husband spread out on the floor as if dead.

"Who are you and what have you done to my husband and where are you taking our tree?"

By now the tree was slung over his shoulder. The right hand appeared as if it was fused to the tree.

Again in response to Gertrude's question the Winter man looked at her with those piercing eyes and turned to the bay window where the tree had rested. The empty tree stand, lights, decorations and the tinsel strewn everywhere.

Upon seeing the devastation he had left, he turned back to Gertrude and Radley and shook his head.

He grabbed at a very small twig, a sapling from the tree which was about six inches long and with his left hand he plucked it from the tree. He then flung it sky ward.

The sapling flew through the air, landing in the tree stand. And pointing his index finger at the young shoot a ball of white lightening came from it. It filled the room with light and smoke as it struck the sapling. All of a sudden the sapling grew and grew into the most marvellous looking tree.

Radley and his mum were absolutely amazed but also terrified at the same time, as they had never seen anything like this before in their lives.

The Winter man then waved his left hand and

made a circular movement and suddenly all the baubles, lights and tinsel flew on to the tree and within seconds it was decorated from head to toe and crowned with a bright shiny star, which Radley and his mum had not seen before.

The Winter man looked admiringly at his handy work and turned to the pair and nodded approvingly.

They both looked on in astonishment.

The Winter man turned to Danny still lying unconscious on the floor and totally unaware as to what was going on. He again pointed his finger at Danny and another bolt of lightning came from his finger and struck Danny hard on the forehead.

Again Gertrude and Danny were amazed and still very frightened but neither felt that he had hurt Danny.

Again the Winter man stared at them with his

piercing eyes and nodded approvingly. He turned toward the lounge door making his way down the hallway to the front door.

Gertrude and Radley stood there in amazement not able to move from fear. The Winter man left through the front door slamming it behind him. He made his way back to the wood carrying the tree with him.

Again no one saw him.

He just moved down Radley's road back across the river and back up into the woods. The snow began to fall and just then the church bell chimed six. Just six hours to Midnight.

When he reached the clearing about ten minutes later, Amy and Calamity were still knelt in the clearing, dutifully waiting for him to return.

They had not moved. Their hearts jumped for joy when they saw him carrying the tree.

The Winter man took the tree and placed it on the stump.

For a single second, which seemed like a lifetime Amy froze thinking that there was no way that the tree would ever be mended.

But Calamity knew better she had every faith in the magic surrounding the wood.

The Winter man held the tree in place and then let go.

The tree stood firm, it had knitted itself back on to the stump, as if it had never been cut.

Both Amy and her mum jumped up from the ground, overjoyed by what they had just seen.

The Winter man fell backwards in the snow, from where he came.

Amy could not believe what she had just seen. "How did it happen mum?"

"It just did Amy. It's magic."

The pair walked back home not talking to each other but just thinking of what had happened.

When they got back home Arthur was back. He had a relieved look on his face. Calamity could tell that he had been worried because he gave them a big smile and an even bigger hug.

"Where have you both been?" He asked. Calamity and Amy began to tell him all about the events of the day.

Arthur sat and listened to them telling him about the Winter man and the tree and how Radley had taken it, and the behaviour of his father.

Arthur was well aware of Danny's appalling behaviour toward his wife and son.

Back at Radley's house, Danny suddenly awoke from his sleep.

He was still lying on the floor where the Winter

man had left him. Radley and Gertrude were kneeling at either side of him.

His eyes opened and he looked up at his wife and son. Gertrude was half expecting him to jump up and become very angry. But no, he just sat up looking around then asked "why am I sat here?"

"Don't you remember dad?"

"No son I don't."

"What time is it?"

"About six thirty Gertrude replied."

"What day is it?"

"It's Christmas Eve dad."

"I don't remember today at all" said Danny.

"I don't think I've had a drink today?"

"No Danny you haven't. But isn't it time you were getting ready to go to the pub?" Gertrude asked.

"I don't really fancy going out tonight. I'd rather

stay in with you two."

"Ok" Gertrude gulped. She was astonished. Danny never stayed in on Christmas Eve, ever.

Gertrude and Radley could not believe how Danny was. They had never known him to be like this. He was always so cranky at the best of times and especially at Christmas. But somehow he appeared to have completely changed after being knocked to the floor by the Winter man.

As the Banks family settled in their home they were sure to have a Christmas like they had never had before.

CHAPTER EIGHT

The Plebs did what they normally did on Christmas Eve. They had their customary meal of cold meats and pickles and had a lovely cosy time, sat by their fire.

But come eleven thirty that evening they got their warm coats on and made their journey to the clearing. But this time Amy was a little scared that the tree would not light up and the Winter man would not appear. And despite her mum saying don't worry, she could not help but feel something would go wrong.

They entered One Tree Wood and took their positions at the side of the clearing so as not to disturb the creatures when they came into the clearing.

At five to midnight the animals started to enter the

clearing. Many of them were the same animals as last Christmas Eve. The tree began to light up on the stroke of the church clock striking midnight and then the Winter man appeared from the ground.

Amy breathed a sigh of relief and in truth so did Calamity and Arthur.

The Winter man rose from the ground picked up a stick and blew his tune while he pranced and danced around the tree. With the animals chanting away and the tree glowing more than ever,

The Plebs remained silent throughout. The Winter man pranced and jumped around the tree. He leapt in the air blowing into the stick furiously.

After ten minutes or so his pace decreased, his jumps decreased and his prancing went to a walk, which became slower and slower around the tree. He then stopped quickly in his tracks but this time he did not fall back into the snowy ground. Instead he looked directly at Amy.

The Winter man moved slowly toward the Plebs, still looking directly at Amy with his deep piercing eyes.

He then turned to Calamity and began to speak in a language that Arthur and Amy could not understand, but clearly Calamity could as she was nodding when the Winter man spoke to her.

Amy and Arthur remained silent whilst the Winter man spoke to Calamity. Wondering of course what he was saying. He then fell silent and never spoke again.

Calamity graciously bowed her head to him and replied "Thank yi sir."

With this the Winter man bowed his head and then turned to walk back to the tree. He turned to face the

Plebs, then fell backwards in the snow and disappeared.

Amy went straight up to her mum and gave her a big hug.

"What did he say Mum?"

"Yes love, what did he say?" Arthur chipped in. Calamity clearly did understand what the Winter man had said. But just turned to the pair of them and said "let's go home. I'll tell you when we get home."

"Oh Mum tell us now."

"Yah go on love."

"No."

"Why mum?"

"Because I'm frozen stiff. I've been stood up in this wood twice today and I'm still freezing from the last time. You know me I don't do cold."

"Ya it is a bit nippy. Let's go home" said Arthur.

Amy sulked a little still itching to know what the Winter man had said but Amy was also freezing too so they all headed for home. At home and over their customary punch and a hot chocolate for Amy, Calamity told them what winter man had said.

She said he had told her that Amy had done wrong for taking Radley to One Tree Wood and said that Radley was wrong for cutting down the tree.

But Calamity was clear to tell Amy that he had said she was right by telling her and they were then able to awaken the Winter man.

Radley had also done the right thing by cutting down the tree because he only wanted to ensure that his mum would not be hurt by his father and this would also mean that he would have a peaceful Christmas. Radley was disloyal to Amy but he was showing his loyalty to his mother. And despite what

Radley had done the Winter man could not condemn him for doing what any loving son would have done.

Amy and Arthur sat quietly and listened to what Calamity had to say. And when she had finished, they reached to her and both hugged her. Amy was so proud of her mum and amazed how she could have done what she did.

"How did you know what the Winter man had said?"
Calamity just smiled and said "I just did Amy!"

"But how did you know to awake the Winter man?"
Calamity said" I just read the instructions in the book love nothing more." Not wanting to make too much of her part in the events of a very long day.

"After all it was the Winter man that did the rest." Then Arthur piped up, "and never mind what ya mum says Amy I think she's brill. Don't you?"

"Yes Dad."

"Why do you think I married her?"

Calamity just smiled back at him and said "right Amy it's bed time."

Amy knew the drill.

"Ok Mum." Amy went up to bed very excited still but very tired and by now feeling very sleepy. She went off to bed and fell asleep within seconds.

And again as always, the Plebs had a great Christmas.

And as for Radley, he too had the best Christmas he had ever had. Because the Winter man had placed a spell on his father. Infact they all had a great time, because Danny never got drunk, or shouted or swore. He never raised his voice or his fists to Radley or Gertrude, the whole of Christmas.

In truth Danny never got angry or upset with his wife or his son ever again. And this all came about because Amy had led Radley to the Secret Tree.

The End

Printed in Great Britain
by Amazon.co.uk, Ltd.,
Marston Gate.